# HERE COMES KATE!

Copyright © 1989 American Teacher Publications

Published by Raintree Publishers

All rights reserved. No part of this book may be reproduced or utilized in any form or by any means, electronic or mechanical, including photocopying, recording, or by any information storage and retrieval system without permission in writing. Inquiries should be addressed to Raintree Publishers, 310 West Wisconsin Avenue, Milwaukee, Wisconsin 53203.

Library of Congress number: 89-3573

**Library of Congress Cataloging in Publication Data.**

Carlson, Judy.
  Here comes Kate!

  (Real readers)
  Summary: A girl in a wheelchair learns when to go fast and when to slow down.
  [1. Wheelchairs—Fiction.  2. Physically handicapped—Fiction]  I. Kibbee, Gordon, ill.  II. Title.  III. Series.
PZ7.C216626He  1989  [E]                                              89-3573
ISBN 0-8172-3515-9

1 2 3 4 5 6 7 8 9 0     93 92 91 90 89

REAL READERS

# HERE COMES KATE!

by Judy Carlson
illustrated by Gordon Kibbee

Westfield Public Library
Westfield, IN 46074

**Raintree Publishers**
Milwaukee

Kate was fast, fast, fast. In her wheelchair, she could zip down the sidewalk as fast as a race car. Zip! There went Kate!

"Want to race?" she asked her friends. When they raced down the hill, Kate would win.

Yes, Kate was fast.

But sometimes she was <u>too</u> fast. She just could not go slow.

"Kate, try and slow down. Oh no! There goes my birdhouse!" her brother Bruce said.

CRASH!

When Kate called, "Here I come!" all her friends ran to get out of Kate's way. She raced along the streets and down driveways. Sometimes things got in her way. When they did CRASH! Outside, she crashed into trash cans, rose beds, and piles of leaves.

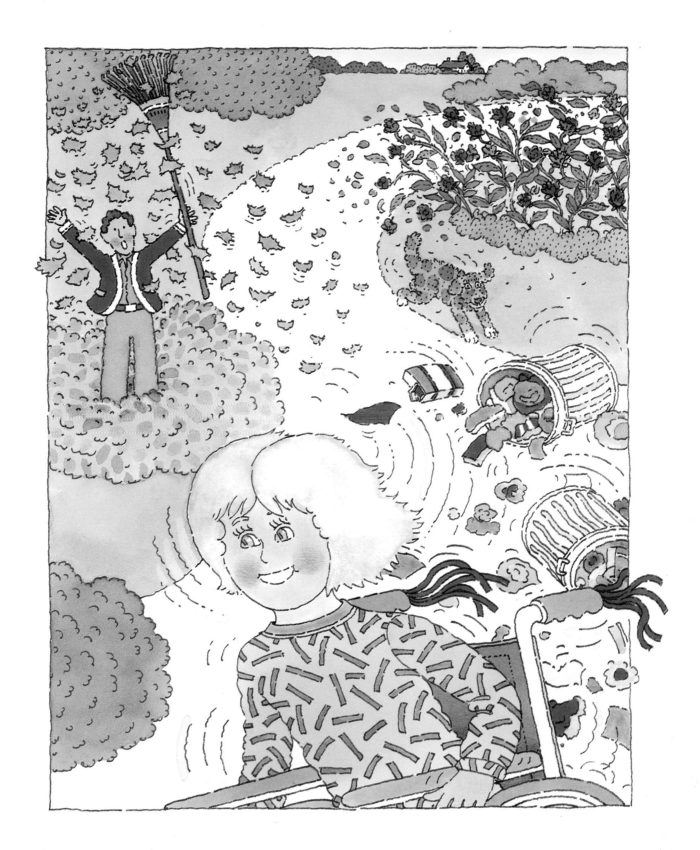

Inside, she was just as bad. She would tip over chairs and crash into beds. She just could not go slow!

"We know that going fast makes you happy," Kate's mom said.

Her dad said, "But we can't be happy when the chairs crack and the beds shake. So, please, slow down!"

"Think slow," said Bruce.

Kate would try to think slow. But sometimes she still went too fast. She just could not go slow!

One day Kate saw a race on TV. This race had wheelchair racers in it. They were fast! They blasted down the streets, their wheels flashing.

Kate rushed outside and raced up and down. CRASH! She ran into the roses and the birdhouse Bruce had just fixed.

"KATE!" her dad yelled. "My roses!"

"KATE!" Bruce yelled. "You broke my birdhouse again!"

"Sorry!" said Kate. And she was! But what could she do? She just could not go slow!

Westfield Public Library
Westfield, IN 46074

That night when Kate was in bed, her mom came in.

"Kate, there's a time to be fast and a time to be slow," her mom said.

"I know," said Kate.

"You know, if you could find a way to slow down at home, we could go to some races and meet some real wheelchair racers," her mom said.

"Wow!" said Kate. "They may have some tips for me! And maybe someday I could be in a wheelchair race!"

So Kate had to think of a way that she could slow down. And she did.

"What a good plan!" her mom said when Kate told her.

Kate and her mom worked all the next day on Kate's plan. Her dad and Bruce laughed when they saw what Kate and her mom had made. There were signs all over the house. They said, "SLOW!" "2 MPH" "STOP!"

"If I go too fast, Mom will give me a ticket," Kate said.

"But if Kate can go two weeks without getting a ticket, I will take her to some real races," said her mom.

"Then I can find out all about wheelchair racing!" Kate said.

Kate did get to go to the races. With the signs to help her, Kate could go slow and stop when she had to. (And some of her new racing friends gave her tips on how to stop on a dime!)

Now Kate races just at the right times and in the right places. She calls to her friends, "Who wants to race? Let's go!"

And then zip, zip, zip—Here comes Kate!

## Sharing the Joy of Reading

Beginning readers enjoy reading books on their own. Reading a book is a worthwhile activity in and of itself for a young reader. However, a child's reading can be even more rewarding if it is shared. This sharing can enhance your child's appreciation — both of the book and of his or her own abilities.

Now that your child has read **Here Comes Kate!**, you can help extend your child's reading experience by encouraging him or her to:

- Retell the story or key concepts presented in this story in his or her own words. The retelling can be oral or written.

- Create a picture of a favorite character, event, or concept from this book.

- Express his or her own ideas and feelings about the characters in this book and other things the characters might do.

Here is a special activity that you and your child can do together to further extend the appreciation of this book: You and your child can make a sign together that will help him or her to remember something. For example, you could make a sign to help your child remember to make his or her bed in the morning. The sign could include a picture of your child making the bed, as well as words. Put the sign up in an appropriate place.

Westfield Public Library
Westfield, IN 46074

jR      Carlson, Judy
CA      Here Comes Kate!    copy 2

DATE DUE

Discarded By
Westfield Public Library

Westfield Public Library
Westfield, IN 46074

WESTFIELD PUBLIC LIBRARY

7 8292 000059809

$1.00 Fine for Removing
the Bar Code Label!!

DEMCO